Make a Million with

ANT and BEE

1,000,000

written and illustrated by Angela Banner

EGMONT

This **ANT and BEE** *book*

belongs to

. . . .

. . . .

One day Ant and Bee wanted
to play . . .

. . . but all the toys

. . . were broken.

. . . and Ant said they could not play ping-pong with only 1 bat.

Bee said they could not
cards with only 1 card

Ant could not walk on 1 stilt,
nor Bee knit with only 1 needle.

They could not play with 1 bit
of jigsaw or 1 marble.

There was nothing to play with!

There was nought . . . 0 . . . nothing!

Ant said they must make some

new toys.

Bee said that they would need

glue . . . string . . . paper and wood.

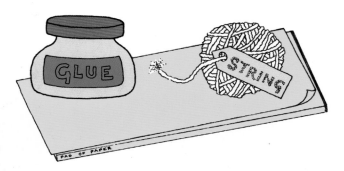

Ant and Bee found some glue
and string and paper . . . and
lots of old paintbrushes made
of wood.

Ant said there must be
a million bits of wood.

Bee said there were not
a million bits of wood.

Ant said they must count
the bits of wood.

Ant and Bee counted all the bits
of wood into piles of ten.

Ant counted ten . . . twenty . . .
thirty . . . forty . . . fifty bits
of wood.

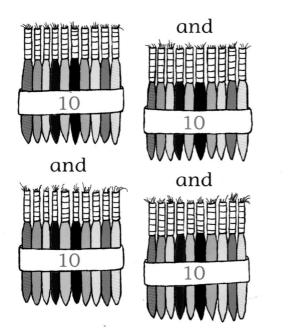

10

and

10

and

10

and

10

and

10

makes

50

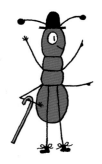

Then Bee counted ten . . .
twenty . . . thirty . . . forty . . .
fifty bits of wood.

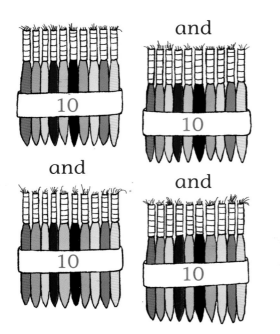

and

and

10

and

and

makes
50

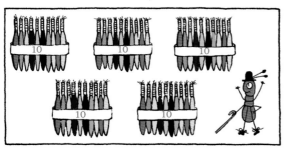

50

and

50

makes . . .

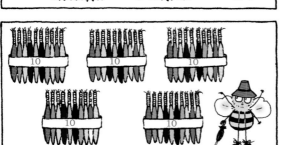

100 bits

of wood.

Ant and Bee thought about
what they could make with
100 bits of wood.

Then Ant and Bee said
they could make a raft.

25

Ant wished Bee had counted
a million bits of wood.

But Bee said . . .

	1	0
	1	0
	1	0
	1	0
	1	0
	1	0
	1	0
	1	0
	1	0
	1	0
1	0	0

. . . his sum showed only
100 bits of wood.

Bee said there were not
a million bits of wood.

Suddenly . . .

. . . Ant began to argue with Bee
about how to make a raft.

So Bee said they must share the 100 bits of wood.

Then Ant could make a raft and Bee could make a raft.

Ant and Bee shared the 100 bits of wood equally between them.

Ant had 50 bits of wood and Bee had 50 bits of wood.

Because 50

and   50
        _____
makes   100

Then Bee slowly made his raft with his 50 bits of wood and lots of string tied into knots.

Ant laughed and laughed and said . . . "So many knots may be strong but knots are trouble and look all wrong."

Then Ant went to make his raft.

Ant broke all his 50 bits of
wood in half . . . and then Ant
had 100 bits of WOOD.

Because 50
and   50
makes   100

Ant made his raft with 100 bits of wood and lots of glue and paper.

Ant made paddle wheels and a sail for his raft.

Ant laughed and laughed and said . . . "I made my raft quickly and stickily!"

Bee had a raft.

TO THE WATER →

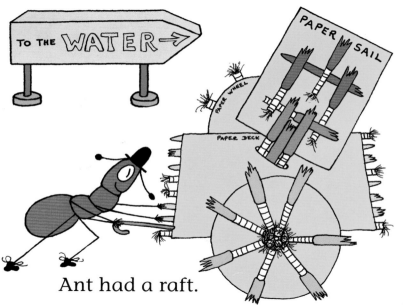

Ant had a raft.

41

When the rafts were on the water Ant laughed and laughed and said . . . "My raft is fast and has a mast!"

Suddenly Ant began to shout . . . "Help! Help! Bee, save me! Bee, save me!"

Ant made a lot of noise because his raft was sinking!

Ant had used glue to make his raft and the glue had washed away!

Bee saved Ant!

Then Bee laughed and laughed and said . . . "Your raft was fast but did not last!"

Then Bee said they must make a bridge over the water so his raft could go under a bridge.

Ant said they must make the bridge with a million stones.

So Ant and Bee went to find a million stones.

Ant and Bee found lots of stones.
Ant said there must be a million
stones . . . so Bee said they must
put the stones into piles.

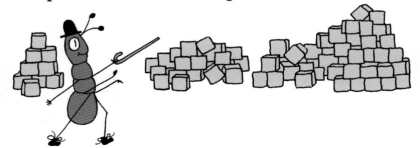

Ant and Bee put a hundred
stones in each pile.

100
STONES

53

Ant said there must be

a million stones.

Bee said there were a thousand

stones because . . .

	1	0	0
	1	0	0
	1	0	0
	1	0	0
	1	0	0
	1	0	0
	1	0	0
	1	0	0
	1	0	0
	1	0	0
1	0	0	0

. . . his sum showed
only 1,000 stones.

Bee said there were
not a million stones.

Ant began to argue with Bee about how to build a bridge.

SO Bee said they must share the 1,000 stones . . . then Ant could build half a bridge and Bee could build half a bridge.

Ant and Bee shared the 1,000 stones equally between them.

Ant had 500 stones and Bee had 500 stones.

Because 500

and 500

makes 1000

Ant wanted to make his half of the bridge with mud and stones.

Bee wanted to make his half of the bridge with string and wood and stones.

Then Ant began to make

his half of the bridge.

And Bee began to make

his half of the bridge.

Then Ant and Bee were pleased with their big bridge made of 1,000 stones.

Ant and Bee ran about on the bridge laughing and laughing and said . . . "The best bridge you ever did see was made by Ant and made by Bee."

Suddenly Ant began to shout . . .
"HELP! HELP! BEE, SAVE ME!
BEE, SAVE ME!"

Ant made a lot of noise because
the rain had made the mud on
the stones slip. Ant's half of the
bridge was falling down!

Bee saved Ant!

Then Ant said . . . "The silliest bridge you ever did see nearly fell on top of me!"

Then Ant and Bee flew away to find a million things that would make a million toys.

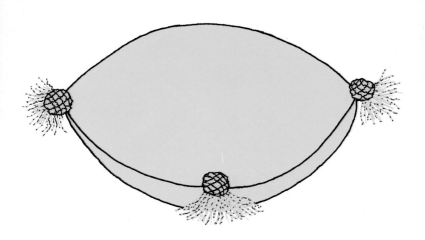

Ant and Bee found a cushion . . .

. . . and ten thousand pins.

Bee said a cushion with 10,000 pins in it would be the biggest pincushion in the world . . . but Ant said NO as 10,000 was not a million.

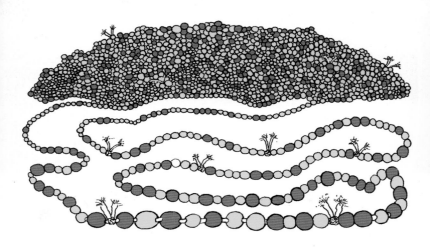

Then Ant and Bee found

a hundred thousand beads.

Bee said 100,000 beads must
make the longest necklace in
the world . . . but Ant said NO
as 100,000 was not a million.

Ant wanted to find a million things, but Bee was tired of looking for a MILLION things.

1,000,000?

Ant asked Bee to count to 1,000,000.

But Bee was sleepy and did not want to count to 1,000,000.

So Ant said he would count to 1,000,000.

Then Bee went to sleep.

BUT when Bee woke up . . .

Ant had only counted to 300.

So Bee went to sleep again.

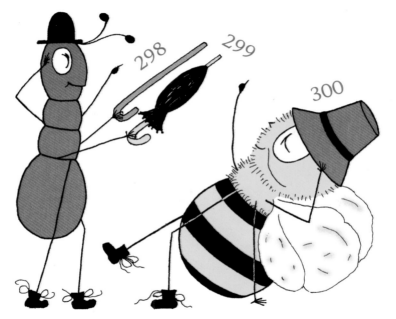

298 299 300

BUT the next time Bee woke up,
Ant told Bee that he had found
a million things!

1,000,000 things!

Then Ant showed Bee . . .

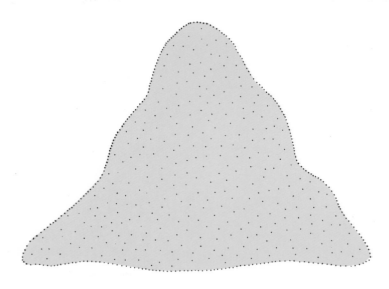

. . . a big pile of sand.

Ant said there were
a million grains of sand!
1,000,000 grains of sand!
Bee picked up 1 grain of
sand and said . . .

"YES! I will not bother to count, as I know that your big pile of sand must be made of a MILLION grains of sand!"

Then Ant and Bee made the
biggest sandcastle in the world
with a million grains of sand.

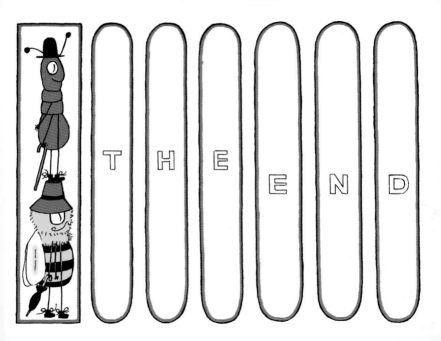

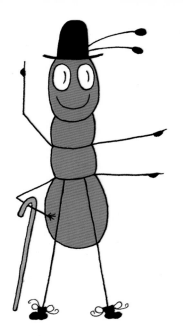

1 million seconds (1,000,000)

= about 11.5 days.

89

1 billion seconds (1,000,000,000)
= about 31.5 years.

That's about the age of the
Zoo Man.

1 trillion seconds

(1,000,000,000,000)

= about 31,500 years.

People were living in

caves this many years ago!